It's a Zingy, Za

Mr. Zuckerman returned to the candy library at Zuckerman's Zonked Candy Factory.

"Here you go, children," he said to Nancy and her class. He passed out bulging bags of candy. "A few treats for everybody. Now, let me put my coat back on, and I'll walk you to the door."

Carefully Mr. Zuckerman slipped on his white coat. Then he led the class back through the factory.

They were just passing the Teensy-Tiny Nut 'n' Fluff table when Mr. Zuckerman slipped a hand into his coat pocket.

"What!" he shouted. He began shoving his hands into every one of his coat pockets. He checked his suit pockets, too. Then his face went white.

"My secret recipe!" he cried. "My fortune. It's gone!"

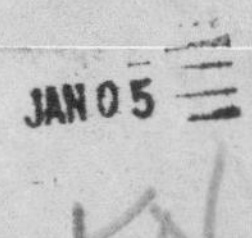

The Nancy Drew Notebooks

- # 1 The Slumber Party Secret
- # 2 The Lost Locket
- # 3 The Secret Santa
- # 4 Bad Day for Ballet
- # 5 The Soccer Shoe Clue
- # 6 The Ice Cream Scoop
- # 7 Trouble at Camp Treehouse
- # 8 The Best Detective
- # 9 The Thanksgiving Surprise
- #10 Not Nice on Ice
- #11 The Pen Pal Puzzle
- #12 The Puppy Problem
- #13 The Wedding Gift Goof
- #14 The Funny Face Fight
- #15 The Crazy Key Clue
- #16 The Ski Slope Mystery
- #17 Whose Pet Is Best?
- #18 The Stolen Unicorn
- #19 The Lemonade Raid
- #20 Hannah's Secret
- #21 Princess on Parade
- #22 The Clue in the Glue
- #23 Alien in the Classroom
- #24 The Hidden Treasures
- #25 Dare at the Fair
- #26 The Lucky Horseshoes
- #27 Trouble Takes the Cake
- #28 Thrill on the Hill
- #29 Lights! Camera! Clues!
- #30 It's No Joke!
- #31 The Fine-Feathered Mystery
- #32 The Black Velvet Mystery
- #33 The Gumdrop Ghost
- #34 Trash or Treasure?
- #35 Third-Grade Reporter
- #36 The Make-Believe Mystery
- #37 Dude Ranch Detective
- #38 Candy Is Dandy
- #39 The Chinese New Year Mystery
- #40 Dinosaur Alert!
- #41 Flower Power
- #42 Circus Act
- #43 The Walkie-Talkie Mystery
- #44 The Purple Fingerprint
- #45 The Dashing Dog Mystery
- #46 The Snow Queen's Surprise

THE NANCY DREW NOTEBOOKS®

#38

Candy Is Dandy

CAROLYN KEENE
ILLUSTRATED BY JAN NAIMO JONES

Aladdin Paperbacks
New York London Toronto Sydney Singapore

First Aladdin Paperbacks edition February 2002
First Minstrel Books edition October 2000

ALADDIN PAPERBACKS
An imprint of Simon & Schuster
Children's Publishing Division
1230 Avenue of the Americas
New York, NY 10020

The text of this book was set in Excelsior.

Printed in the United States of America
10 9 8 7 6 5 4

ISBN 0-671-04269-6

1

A Tasty Trip

Nancy Drew stared out the school bus window. “When will we get there?” she said.

“I know. I can’t wait,” agreed Nancy’s best friend Bess Marvin. She was sitting in the seat right behind Nancy. “A class field trip to Zuckerman’s Zonked Candy Factory. My wildest dreams are coming true!”

“Yeah! All the candy we can eat,” said Bess’s cousin George Fayne. She was sitting next to Nancy.

Bess and George were as different as two cousins could be. Brown-haired

George was tall and loved sports. Bess had long blond hair. She didn't like to do anything that made her dirty or sweaty. But both cousins loved candy.

Everybody else in the girls' third-grade class was excited about the field trip, too. Over the chatter of the other kids, Bess announced, "Nobody's going to eat more candy than me on this field trip!"

"Oh, yeah?" yelled a voice a few seats back. It was Josie Blanton. She had the sweetest of all the sweet tooths at Carl Sandburg Elementary.

"I'll have you beat easy, Bess," Josie said. "I even made a candy-eating plan. See?"

Josie held up her notebook. It had a peppermint pink cover. She opened it. On one page she had printed:

1) Start with the heavy stuff—chocolates and caramels.
2) Exercise the jaws with jelly bears and taffy.
3) Go for anything super-sour.
4) Finish with long-lasting mints and an all-day sucker.

"You're the only person I know who studies for a field trip, Josie," George said. She rolled her brown eyes.

"Hey, I take my candy seriously," Josie answered. "When I grow up, I want to have a candy factory just like Zuckerman's Zonked. Ow!"

The bus had lurched to a halt. Josie, who was standing when she should have been sitting, bonked her nose on the seat in front of her. She rubbed her nose grumpily.

But when she glanced out the window, her scowl turned into a laugh. "Wow!" she yelled.

Nancy looked, too. She squealed with delight. Zuckerman's Zonked Candy Factory was a tall brick building. It would have looked ordinary, except every brick was painted a different color of the rainbow.

"The bricks look like jelly beans!" Bess exclaimed, licking her lips.

"I can't wait to see the inside!" George shouted.

All the kids tumbled into the bus aisle.

They clapped their hands and jumped up and down in excitement.

"Single file, children," called their teacher, Mrs. Reynolds. Then she led the class off the bus and through the factory's front door. The door looked like a big, smiling mouth.

"Wow, I feel like I'm being swallowed by a giant," Josie said. She shivered gleefully as she walked beneath some huge white teeth.

"Now I know what a chocolate bar feels like," Bess joked.

The factory was even more wonderful inside. Nancy gasped as she gazed at a large, open room filled with candy-making contraptions.

There were giant, gleaming steel pots with steam bubbling out of them. Moving belts carried chocolate bars from one end of the big room to the other. Lined up against a wall were enormous plastic containers. They were filled with sugar, cocoa, and caramel. The air was filled with a delicious smell.

"Hey, look at that," Bess said excitedly.

"They're making one of my favorite candy bars right over there." She pointed to a corner. Workers in white jumpsuits and hats were busy wrapping creamy squares of candy in rainbow-colored foil.

"I recognize that wrapper," Nancy said. "Those are Karamel Krunchettes."

"Ooh, look at *that* thing!" George exclaimed.

She was pointing at a big steel tub. Sticking out of the side of the tub was a long silver spout. Pouring out of the spout was a stream of bright purple goo. More factory workers were catching the goo in trays with small shapes punched into them.

"Those must be the molds for Zuckerman's Sticky Jelly Bugs," Andrew Leoni said. Andrew was one of the boys in Nancy's class. He liked anything as long as it was extra yucky.

"Sticky Jelly Bugs are the coolest," Andrew said.

"Yeah," Jason Hutchings said. He was standing next to Andrew. "Zuckerman's

Sticky Jelly Bugs are way stickier than plain old jelly bears. If you throw a Sticky Jelly Bug at the wall, *or* at a girl, it will stick just like a real fly!"

Jason's friends Mike Minelli and David Berger giggled. All three boys began to flap their arms. Jason stuck out his tongue.

"Buzzzzzzz," Mike said.

"Lookit, we're Sticky Jelly Bugs!" David yelled.

"Ick!" Bess cried.

George rolled her eyes and muttered, "Boys are so gross!"

Just then a man burst through a nearby doorway. He wore a wrinkled brown suit that matched his smiling, light brown eyes. His hair was gray and wild. It stuck out from his head in big, curly tufts. He was carrying a white canvas bag.

"Children!" the man cried. "Welcome to my factory. I am your host, Mr. Zuckerman."

Mr. Zuckerman gave a deep bow. His fuzzy gray curls bounced. Then he looked up, winked at the children, and straightened his baggy suit.

"Time for the grand tour," Mr. Zuckerman announced. "But first we must get dressed."

He reached into his bag and pulled out a bunch of hats. They were the same white caps the factory workers were wearing. They were soft and bunchy, like shower caps. Moving from child to child, Mr. Zuckerman quickly passed out all the hats.

"Hey," Andrew called. "You gave me three of these funny caps. But I've only got one head."

"Right you are," Mr. Zuckerman said. "I want you to put one of the caps over your hair. Then put the other two over your shoes, as I'm doing."

Mr. Zuckerman wrapped the caps around his shoes. They made his feet looked like puffy white pillows. Then the factory owner placed his last cap over his fuzzy hair. Finally he put on a long white jacket that looked like a doctor's coat.

The kids had to giggle at Mr. Zuckerman's strange outfit. Of course, once they put on their own shower caps, they looked just as funny as he did.

"Laugh if you will, kiddies, but this is to keep our factory as clean as possible," Mr. Zuckerman said. "You may not know it, but you carry all sorts of dust, dirt, and other bad stuff in your clothes and hair."

Bess peered at the ends of her shiny blond hair. "But I just had a shampoo last night," she said with a pout.

"Even so," Mr. Zuckerman replied, "we have to keep our factory squeaky-clean. That's why I wear my white coat here and the workers wear their jumpsuits."

Mr. Zuckerman walked to the huge tub of purple goo. He pointed at the silver tub. It practically glimmered under the bright factory lights.

"You see?" he said, turning to Nancy's class. "At Zuckerman's Zonked we take pride in a *sparkling* clean factory."

Mr. Zuckerman grinned and threw his arms out wide.

CLANK!

"Oh!" Mr. Zuckerman exclaimed. One of his hands had smacked into the goo spout.

Nancy gasped as she watched the goo tub begin to spin around in a circle. The spout spun with it. Purple goo streamed from the spout as it whirled around. It sprayed a wide splash of sticky goo on the floor.

"Eeek!" the kids cried, scrambling away from the stream of goo.

Finally the tub stopped spinning—when the goo spout collided with Mr. Zuckerman.

"Oof!" the factory owner cried. A waterfall of warm purple goo gushed onto his shirt. It coated his white coat and his tie. It covered his pants. It drenched his feet.

"Talk about sweet," Josie whispered. She looked a little jealous. "You know, *I* wouldn't mind being covered in candy from head to toe."

But Mr. Zuckerman was far from pleased.

"Oh, no!" he cried. He gazed at his

sticky suit in dismay. A crowd of factory workers rushed to his aid with wet towels. Mrs. Reynolds tried to help, too.

As the helpers mopped at Mr. Zuckerman's clothes, he said to the children, "That was a batch of our Zuckerman's *Sooper* Sticky Jelly Bug goo! Oh, it will take days to un-gum myself."

Mr. Zuckerman rolled his eyes and said, "And just when I was going to tell you about my big secret!"

2

Zuckerman's Secret

"Secret!" Nancy whispered to Bess. "What could it be?" She waited for Mr. Zuckerman to say something else. But he only grumbled and dabbed at his clothes with a towel. Bess giggled when the towel stuck to Mr. Zuckerman's coat.

"When I make sticky candy, it *really* sticks," Mr. Zuckerman said. Then he shrugged and turned to the class. "Oh, well. On with the tour, children."

Nancy bit her lip. "But what about the secret?" she whispered to George.

"Maybe we can remind him at the end of the tour," George whispered back.

The kids followed Mr. Zuckerman through a maze of candy-making machines. He stopped in front of a metal arm with a pointy end.

"Here's the peanut-butter squirter," Mr. Zuckerman said. He took a tray of small chocolate balls and placed it beneath the arm. Then he pressed a button. The arm began shooting gobs of peanut butter into the balls of chocolate.

"That's the coolest thing ever!" George gasped.

Next Mr. Zuckerman led the class to a row of many small pots. Inside the pots were pretty rainbow-colored liquids.

"This is the coloring for our Hundred-Color Jawbreakers," Mr. Zuckerman said with a chuckle. "They were one of my own inventions, I'm proud to say."

Then Mr. Zuckerman moved on to a big pot of melted marshmallows. He plucked a tiny chocolate square off a nearby table.

"Ah, and this is a new candy," he announced. "You'll see it in the stores in the next few months."

"Hey!" Josie exclaimed. "That chocolate is shaped like a little slice of bread."

"Right you are," Mr. Zuckerman said with a grin. "I'm calling the candy Teensy-Tiny Nut 'n' Fluffs. They're little sandwiches of chocolate bread, whipped marshmallow, and peanut butter."

"Yum!" Bess squealed. She jumped up and down.

"Oh, does that sound good to you?" Mr. Zuckerman said with a twinkle in his eye. "You know, I haven't got the recipe *just* right yet. That's why we have a special tasting area."

He led the class to a small room with a big table in the middle of it. It was piled high with candy—including Teensy-Tiny Nut 'n' Fluffs. Bess gasped with joy.

"I have to eat a lot of sweets to make sure the recipes are just right," Mr. Zuckerman said. "Usually I do all of the candy tasting myself. But sometimes I need help."

"Say no more!" Josie cried. She ran to the table and popped a Teensy-Tiny Nut 'n' Fluff into her mouth.

"Oh, Mr. Zuckerman," she said with her mouth full. "I think this recipe is just perfect!"

"I'll see about that," Bess said. She ran to Josie's side and gobbled one of the little sandwiches. "Delicious!" she said.

The rest of the kids quickly joined in.

"Oh, look. A Zonked Licorice Snake!" Andrew Leoni cried. He picked a black, scary-looking snake off the table. Then he bit off its head.

George curled her lip at Andrew.

"Yuck!" she exclaimed. "Why would you eat a snake when you can have a set of Frostee Jewels instead?" She grabbed a necklace of pretty pink and blue candies off the pile on the table. She nibbled one of the jewels before putting on the necklace.

"You said it!" Nancy said. She was licking a Cherry Baby, a red lollipop in the shape of a baby.

"Please finish your candy before we go to the next room, children," Mr. Zuckerman said. "It's the most special room of all."

"What could be better than the candy-tasting room?" Bess asked. She licked whipped marshmallow off her fingers.

The class followed Mr. Zuckerman down a hallway. The hall had many twists and turns to it. On the wall were pictures of Zuckerman's Zonked candies.

"Look, those are Quake Puffs," Jason Hutchings said. He pointed to one of the pictures. "They fizz and explode in your mouth. They're so cool!"

"My favorite is Zoobers," Josie retorted. She pointed to a picture of animal-shaped chocolate chews.

"Zoobers are okay," Mike Minelli said. "But I like Zuckerman's Chocolate Eyeballs the best."

"If it's gross, you can bet Mike Minelli will eat it," George said.

Finally the group arrived at a big wooden door.

"Here we are," Mr. Zuckerman said, throwing the door open.

The kids found themselves peering into a beautiful library. In the middle of the room stood a big wooden table and some matching chairs. The shelves along the walls were filled with old books. There were big books and little books and books with candy-colored covers.

"Books!" Andrew said, sounding mad. "Awww, where's the candy?"

"Without these books, there would be no candy," Mr. Zuckerman replied. He took off his sticky white coat and carefully hung it over the back of a chair. Then he took some books off the shelves. He laid them on the table so the children could see them.

"These are my treasured candy cookbooks," Mr. Zuckerman said. "Many of them were written by my grandfather Abraham Zuckerman. He was the one who opened Zuckerman's Zonked Candy Factory. That was back in 1925."

"Wow!" Josie said. "Maybe someday when I'm a candy maker, I'll have a library like this."

Mr. Zuckerman reached onto a high shelf for some very large books. They were bound in a creamy brown leather. "Here's my grandfather's best work—his chocolate encyclopedia. It covers every Zuckerman's Zonked chocolate treat, from Abe's Almond Bars to Zoobers."

Bess raised her hand. When Mr. Zuckerman called on her, she asked, "Did you write any of these recipe books, Mr. Zuckerman?"

"Indeed I did," Mr. Zuckerman said. "You see, crazy new candy recipes are a Zuckerman family tradition. I'm always trying to come up with exciting new treats. In fact, I was going to tell you about my latest brainstorm, wasn't I?"

"This must be the secret he was talking about," Nancy whispered to George.

"Children, I have dreamed up an incredible new candy," Mr. Zuckerman said proudly. "It is the perfect sweet! It's sure to make me millions."

"What is it?" Josie blurted, forgetting to raise her hand first.

Mr. Zuckerman walked over to his white coat on the chair. He reached into the coat pocket and pulled out a crumpled piece of paper. He waved the paper in the air.

“Here it is—the secret formula,” he said. “This candy will be as creamy as chocolate and as chewy as caramel. It’s as long-lasting as an all-day sucker. And if you bite down on it, it squirts neon colors onto your tongue. I’ve almost got the recipe just right. You see, the trick is in the maple syrup. Then you . . .”

Mr. Zuckerman stopped talking and laughed. “Well, I can’t give away my secret recipe, can I? You’ll taste it soon enough, children. But for now, look but don’t touch.”

He held the paper in the air for a moment. Then he stuffed it back into the pocket of his white coat.

“Well, I think we’ve seen enough of the library,” Mr. Zuckerman said. He picked up the candy cookbooks from the table and put them back on the shelves.

Mrs. Reynolds looked at her watch. Then she said, “Thank you for the wonderful tour, Mr. Zuckerman. It’s time for us to go back to school now.”

“I can’t let you leave without a few goodie bags, can I?” Mr. Zuckerman declared. "I've already packed up some sweets for you. They're in my office. I'll be right back."

Mr. Zuckerman swept out of the library.

"More candy? I can't believe it!" Bess said happily.

While they waited for Mr. Zuckerman, Nancy's classmates drifted to different corners of the library. Nancy wandered over to one wall. She gazed up at the high shelf where Mr. Zuckerman kept the cookbooks with the pretty brown covers.

"What big, beautiful books," Nancy whispered. Then she giggled. "They even look like chocolate."

Just then Mr. Zuckerman returned to the library.

"Here you go, children," he said. He passed out bulging bags of candy. "A few treats for everybody. Now, let me put my coat back on, and I'll walk you to the door."

Carefully Mr. Zuckerman slipped on his sticky coat. Then he led the class back through the factory. They were just passing the Teensy-Tiny Nut 'n' Fluff table when Mr. Zuckerman slipped a hand into his coat pocket.

"What!" he shouted. He stumbled to a stop. He began shoving his hands into every one of his coat pockets. He checked his suit pockets, too. Then his face went white. "My secret recipe!" he cried. "My fortune. It's gone!"

3

A Sticky Mystery

The secret recipe is missing?" Nancy gasped. "I can't believe it."

"What could have happened to it?" Bess cried.

Mr. Zuckerman dropped to his hands and knees. He began searching the factory floor for the missing scrap of paper.

"Where could it be?" he muttered.

"Class," Mrs. Reynolds called, "let's help Mr. Zuckerman look for his recipe."

"Oh, thank you, children," Mr. Zuckerman called. He was crawling next to the big pot of melted marshmallows. "Be careful, though. Stay away from the candy-making machines."

Nancy ducked beneath a table to look for the recipe. She felt around the floor but didn't find a thing. When she popped her head out, she saw all her classmates crawling around the plastic sugar bins or peeking into corners. All of them except Josie Blanton. Josie was standing near the door. She looked as if she was about to cry.

Nancy was wondering what was wrong with Josie when Mr. Zuckerman interrupted her thoughts.

"Has anybody found the recipe?" he called. He pulled himself to his feet.

"Not me," said one of Nancy's classmates.

"Me either!" called another.

"It's no use!" Mr. Zuckerman wailed. "My recipe is gone!"

"I'm sorry we couldn't find it for you, Mr. Zuckerman," Mrs. Reynolds said.

"Oh, you did your best." The frazzled factory owner sighed. Sad, he walked the class to the school bus.

Soon after the kids had settled into their bus seats, they began to chatter about the missing recipe.

"Where could it have gone?" George wondered. She twirled one of her dark brown curls around her finger thoughtfully.

Bess opened her blue eyes wide. "You don't think somebody stole it, do you?" she asked Nancy.

Nancy didn't answer. She was too busy staring at Josie Blanton. Josie was sitting in the seat in front of hers. She was chewing on a chocolate bar, but she didn't seem very interested in it. She gazed out the window. And she didn't talk to anybody about the missing recipe.

"Hmmm," Nancy said. "I wonder . . ."

But before Nancy could say how suspicious Josie looked, the bus arrived at their school, Carl Sandburg Elementary.

"There's my mom," George said. She pointed at Mrs. Fayne's car parked in front of the school. "Remember, Nancy, she's giving us a ride to soccer practice.

We'd better hurry. We don't want to be late."

George and Nancy said goodbye to Bess and ran off the bus.

In a short while Nancy was on the soccer field, practicing her dribbling and punts. She was playing so hard that she forgot all about Josie and the missing recipe.

Before she knew it, Coach Santos called out, "Okay, girls. Good job today. Time to go home."

"Really?" George said. She bounced a soccer ball on her knee. "I could practice all night."

"Not me," Nancy said. She wiped her forehead with her sleeve. "I'm going home for a snack. See you tomorrow, George."

Nancy was enjoying her walk home when something made her stop. A delicious smell filled the air.

"Mmm," Nancy whispered. She closed her eyes. "That smell reminds me of Hannah's pancakes."

When she opened her eyes, she realized

she was standing in front of Josie Blanton's house. A front window was open. Through the window, Nancy could see Josie's kitchen. Josie and her mother were standing at the counter, stirring something in a big mixing bowl.

Josie grinned. Then she stuck her finger in the mixing bowl and licked some batter off her finger. She only giggled when her mother scolded her.

Next Josie's mother took a spoon and began dropping the batter onto a baking sheet. Nancy sniffed the air again. Then her mouth dropped open.

"Now I recognize that smell," she said. "It's maple syrup."

Suddenly Nancy remembered what Mr. Zuckerman had said about his candy recipe: "The trick is in the maple syrup."

Nancy ran the rest of the way home.

"Hannah!" Nancy called when she burst through the kitchen door.

Hannah was at the counter, cutting up vegetables for supper. "What's all the commotion, Nancy?" Hannah said. She wiped her hands on a dish towel.

"I have to make a call," Nancy said breathlessly. "Can you please help me look up a number in the phone book?"

"Of course, dear," Hannah said. She pulled the telephone book out of one of the kitchen drawers.

"I need the number for Zuckerman's Zonked Candy Factory," Nancy said.

Hannah flipped through the *Z*'s and said, "Here it is—555–ZONK."

Nancy punched in the number. After three rings a weary voice answered. Nancy recognized it as Mr. Zuckerman's. "Zuckerman's Zonked," he said sadly.

"Hello, Mr. Zuckerman? This is Nancy Drew," said Nancy. "I was one of the kids on the field trip at your factory today."

"Oh. Oh, yes, dear," Mr. Zuckerman said. "What can I do for you, young lady?"

"I wanted to know if you've found your secret recipe," Nancy said.

"Well, as a matter of fact, I haven't," Mr. Zuckerman said. He sounded very upset. "I just can't imagine what's happened to it. It was stupid of me to keep only one copy of the recipe. And now it's lost. I've looked everywhere, but it's nowhere to be found."

"I think that's because somebody may have taken it," Nancy said.

"What!" Mr. Zuckerman sputtered. "But who would do a thing like that? And why?"

"That's what I'm going to find out, Mr. Zuckerman," Nancy said.

Nancy bit her lip and thought to herself, *In fact, I think I already know.*

"I promise I'll call you as soon as I learn something," Nancy told Mr. Zuckerman. Then she hung up the phone and went to her room.

Nancy opened her backpack and took out the shiny blue notebook where she always wrote down the clues to her mysteries. She turned to a clean page and wrote "The Mystery of the Missing Candy Recipe. Chief suspect: Josie Blanton."

4

Josie's Plan

The next morning Nancy ran into her classroom. Bess and George were already there. Nancy hurried over to her best friends.

"Guess what?" Nancy whispered. "I'm not sure if Mr. Zuckerman lost his candy recipe. I think somebody might have taken it."

Then she told Bess and George all about what she'd seen the day before.

"When I was walking home from soccer practice, I passed Josie's house," Nancy whispered. "Josie and her mother were cooking in the kitchen."

"That doesn't seem too strange," Bess said.

"They were baking something that smelled just like maple syrup," Nancy said.

"What's the big deal about that?" George asked. "Everybody knows that Josie loves anything sweet."

"Remember what Mr. Zuckerman said about his recipe, though?" Nancy said. "The secret ingredient was maple syrup!"

Bess looked upset. "Do you really think Josie took the recipe?" she asked. "I mean, Josie does love candy. Yesterday at the candy factory, she ate enough Zuckerman's Peanut Butter-O's to feed ten squirrels. She licked so many Zonked Wacky Fruitz, her tongue turned bright purple. But I can't see Josie stealing."

"I thought so, too," Nancy said sadly. "But then I remembered what Josie said on the bus. She said she wants to open her own candy factory someday."

"Maybe this is how she'll get her start," George whispered.

"Girls," Mrs. Reynolds called. "It's time to stop talking and get to work. The assignment for the morning is to write a composition about our trip to Zuckerman's Zonked Candy Factory."

Nancy, Bess, and George hurried to their desks. Nancy pulled a sharp pencil and a piece of paper out of her desk. She chewed on her eraser for a moment, thinking. Then she began to write.

"Going to Zuckerman's Zonked was the best field trip ever. I had fun seeing how my favorite treats are made," she wrote in her neat, straight handwriting. "Mr. Zuckerman seems to love making candy. I think it is sad that his secret recipe was lost. Now we may never get to taste his great new idea."

Nancy looked up from her paper and glanced at Josie, who sat two rows away. Josie was writing busily. I wonder what Josie's writing, Nancy thought. Maybe there's a clue to this mystery in her composition.

Nancy didn't have a chance to talk to Bess and George again until lunchtime.

As the class walked to the cafeteria, Nancy had an idea. "Let's sit next to Josie at lunch," she said to Bess and George. "Maybe she'll give us some clues."

When the girls got to the cafeteria, Josie had already sat down. She was unpacking her lunch when Nancy, Bess, and George joined her. Nancy sat next to Josie, and George sat next to Nancy. Bess sat across from them.

"Hi, guys," Josie said. She unwrapped a gooey, smushy-looking sandwich. "Look what I brought. It's made with peanut butter and whipped marshmallow—just like at Zuckerman's Zonked. Too bad my mom wouldn't dip the bread in chocolate, though."

Bess gaped at Josie's lunch. Josie also had a container of sugar-coated fruity cereal and a pint of chocolate milk.

"I wish my mom let me eat sweets for lunch," Bess said. She pulled out her own ham sandwich, regular milk, and apple and frowned at them. She sighed a big sigh and took a halfhearted bite of the fruit.

Josie had eaten only a bit of her sticky sandwich when suddenly she grinned and declared, "Time for dessert!" She reached into her lunchbox and pulled out something small and round. It was wrapped in aluminum foil. When Josie pulled the foil off, she was holding a creamy candy. It looked like a chocolate, except it was light brown.

Nancy sniffed. The candy smelled strongly of maple syrup.

"What is that, Josie?" Nancy asked. She tried hard not to sound too suspicious.

"Guess," Josie responded with a big grin. Then she popped the candy into her mouth. Suddenly her smile disappeared. Josie's eyes opened wide and started watering. She grabbed her napkin and spit the candy into it.

"Blech!" she cried. Then she folded her arms and frowned.

"Making candy is harder than I thought," she said.

"What do you mean?" Nancy asked.

"When Mr. Zuckerman lost his recipe, I felt so bad for him," Josie answered. "I thought I'd try to surprise him by coming up with a candy recipe to replace his. That's what I wrote about in my essay this morning. My mom and I worked on this candy all afternoon yesterday. We used lots of maple syrup. But Mr. Zuckerman would never make something that tastes as yucky as this."

Josie turned to Nancy. "I guess I'm not quite ready to be a candy maker," she said sadly. "Maybe you should try to come up with the recipe, Nancy."

Nancy patted Josie's shoulder kindly. Then she whispered in George's ear. "Did you hear that?" she asked. "Josie was just trying to *guess* Mr. Zuckerman's recipe. She didn't have it at all."

With her back still turned to Josie, Nancy took her blue clue notebook out of her jeans pocket. She opened it to her Candy Hunt suspect page and crossed out Josie's name. She was closing her notebook when she heard a commotion at the next cafeteria table.

Bess and George were looking over

there, too. "Hmm, what's up with Stevie Sikes?" George asked.

Stevie had black curly hair that never stayed neat. Not that he cared. He was always too busy with his science experiments to worry about things like messy hair. Stevie wanted to be a chemist when he grew up.

He was talking about his latest science project just then. Or rather, he *wasn't* talking about it.

A circle of boys had formed around Stevie. Nancy could hear voices saying, "Hey, Stevie. Tell us! What is it that you're working on?"

"It's top secret," Stevie answered. He folded his arms across his chest and clamped his mouth shut.

"Aw, come on, you can tell us," David Berger said. "What is that stuff you're cooking up?"

"No!" Stevie declared. "All the famous scientists say you should never talk about your research until it's finished. So, no matter how much it bugs all of you, I'll never tell."

With that, Stevie slammed his lunch box shut and jumped up from the table. He stalked to the hall monitor at the cafeteria door. When she gave him a hall pass, he rushed through the door.

Nancy glanced at Bess and George. "Are you thinking what I'm thinking?" she asked.

"Let's go!" Bess said.

The three girls hopped up from the table and raced to the hall monitor.

"My, so many of Mrs. Reynolds's students are walking the halls today." The hall monitor laughed. She gave the girls their hall passes.

"Thank you," Nancy said as they hurried out of the cafeteria. She peered down the long school hallway.

"There's Stevie," she said, pointing to the end of the hallway. She could see Stevie ducking into their own classroom.

The girls walked as fast as they could down the hallway. When they were near their classroom door, Nancy held a finger to her lips. "Shhhh," she warned.

The friends tiptoed to the door and

poked their heads inside. Stevie was at the science station in the back of the room. He held up a plastic beaker. It was filled with pink liquid. He swirled the liquid around and around. He squinted at it. Then he frowned.

Nancy sniffed the air. "Do you smell that?" she whispered.

"It smells sweet," George hissed.

"Mmm," Bess said. "It smells just like cotton candy."

Suddenly Stevie looked up from his experiment. He'd seen them.

"Hey!" he yelled. He scowled and waved his arm at the girls, knocking over a bag at his elbow. White powder spilled out of the bag onto the floor.

"That's sugar," Nancy said.

"Get out of here!" Stevie yelled. "This is secret."

Nancy stuttered, "B-but what are you—"

"Doing here?" A grown-up voice behind Nancy finished her sentence. Nancy whirled around. It was Mrs. Reynolds.

The teacher stepped past Nancy,

George, and Bess and joined Stevie at the science station. Then she smiled and said, "Stevie's working on something very private. Would you girls mind waiting in the cafeteria until the bell rings?"

"Yes, Mrs. Reynolds," Nancy, Bess, and George said meekly. They left the classroom and trudged back toward the cafeteria. They were speechless. At least, for a moment.

Finally Bess sputtered, "I just don't get it. Do you think Stevie is working on Mr. Zuckerman's candy recipe?"

Nancy felt confused and upset. "I don't know yet," she said. "But if he is, then that means Mrs. Reynolds is in on his plan!"

5

Some Suspicious Grown-ups

That afternoon Nancy could barely concentrate on her math worksheets. She sneaked glances at Bess and George. They looked as upset as she was.

Finally the bell rang for the end of the school day. The three girls slumped down the hallway.

"What should we do about Stevie and Mrs. Reynolds?" Bess asked. She stopped walking and looked at Nancy and George sadly.

"I don't know," Nancy said. "I never thought Mrs. Reynolds would do something dishonest."

"Yeah, this is big!" George said.

Nancy pulled her blue notebook out of her backpack. She wrote down the new clue: "Stevie and Mrs. Reynolds working on a sugary secret project."

Nancy pondered the clue for a moment. "This isn't enough to prove that Mrs. Reynolds and Stevie have Mr. Zuckerman's recipe," she said. "But it sure doesn't look good, does it? I'm going to talk to my father about all this when he gets home from work."

"But that's not until dinnertime," George said. "What should we do until then?"

"I don't know about you," Bess said, "but all this upsetting news about Mrs. Reynolds has made me hungry. Let's stop at the Double Dip for an ice-cream cone."

"That does sound good," Nancy said. "Let's call and ask for permission."

After they'd called Hannah, Mrs. Marvin, and Mrs. Fayne from the school pay phone, the girls headed for the Double Dip. As they neared the ice-cream parlor, Bess began to cheer up.

"Maybe I'll get a chocolate sundae with peanut butter and marshmallows," she said. "It will taste just like one of Mr. Zuckerman's Teensy-Tiny Nut 'n' Fluffs."

"That does sound yummy," George said.

"Uh-huh!" Nancy agreed. "On to the Double Dip."

The girls were just across the street from the store when George gasped. She pointed at the Double Dip's big window.

"What is it, George?" Nancy asked.

She followed George's gaze to the ice-cream parlor. Hanging in the window was a freshly painted sign. It was decorated with pictures of chocolate bars and jelly bears. The sign said, "The Double Dip. Serving ice cream, cookies, and now homemade candy!"

"Candy!" Nancy said.

The girls ran across the street and peeked into the Double Dip's window.

"Look next to the cash register," Nancy whispered. She pointed at a glass case filled with creamy chocolates, caramels, and other tasty stuff.

"Do you see anything that looks like it has maple syrup in it?" George asked.

Before Nancy could answer, Bess said, "Hey, look who's buying ice cream. It's Andrew Leoni."

Andrew was standing at the counter. He was talking to the Double Dip's owner, Cathy Perez. She handed him a waffle cone piled high with three scoops of ice cream. Andrew gave her a big grin. He took a lick off the top scoop and shook Cathy's hand. Then he started to walk to the door.

"Hey, Andrew didn't pay for his ice cream," Bess said.

"Quick, let's hide," Nancy said. The girls ran to the corner and ducked behind a mailbox. They hid there until they couldn't see Andrew anymore.

"Why did you want to hide from Andrew, Nancy?" George asked as they stumbled out from behind the mailbox.

"Why would Cathy give Andrew free ice cream?" Nancy said with a frown. "That seemed sort of fishy."

"And on the day she starts selling homemade candy," Bess added.

"Maybe Andrew traded Mr. Zuckerman's secret recipe for a lifetime supply of free scoops," Nancy said.

"You know, suddenly I've lost my appetite for ice cream," George said. She looked troubled.

"Me, too," Nancy said.

"Me, too, I guess," Bess agreed. But she didn't sound as if she meant it.

"All I want to do is talk to my dad about all this," Nancy said as the girls turned toward home. "He'll know what to do."

Nancy said goodbye to her friends. Then slowly and sadly she walked home.

"How was your ice cream?" Hannah asked when Nancy slumped through the back door.

"Not so great," Nancy said. "I think I'll just do homework until dinnertime, Hannah."

Nancy tried her best to do her homework until her father arrived home from his law offices. But she found herself daydreaming more than she was working. When Mr. Drew walked through the door, Nancy had barely looked at the spelling list she was supposed to memorize.

"Hi, Pumpkin, how was your day?" Mr. Drew called from the front hall.

Ever since Nancy was small, her father had called her Pumpkin. That is, when he didn't call her Pudding Pie. Nancy loved both her nicknames.

"Oh, Daddy," she called. "You'll never guess what's happened." She grabbed her clue notebook and ran to give her father a hug. Then she opened her notebook to the missing recipe page. Underneath the clue about Stevie Sikes and Mrs. Reynolds, Nancy had written, "*More* suspects: Andrew Leoni and Cathy Perez."

"I've got too many suspects to handle on my new mystery, Daddy," Nancy said.

"Let's talk about it over dinner," Mr. Drew said as he slipped his briefcase into the hall closet. "Mmm, I smell Hannah's famous roast chicken!"

They sat down at the kitchen table and

dug into plates of chicken and green beans. Then Nancy told her father everything that had happened that day. "At first I thought Josie had the recipe," Nancy said. She took a quick sip of milk. "Then I realized Josie was just trying to help Mr. Zuckerman.

"Next, it looked as if Stevie and Mrs. Reynolds were cooking up Mr. Zuckerman's candy recipe," she continued. "And now Cathy Perez is serving homemade candy, too. Everywhere I go, there's candy, candy, candy. But I don't know who has that recipe!"

"Maybe nobody has it, Pudding Pie," Mr. Drew said. He cut up his chicken and thought a moment. Then he said, "You know the best way to find out the truth, Pumpkin?"

"How?" Nancy asked.

Her father gave her a wink and smiled kindly. "Just ask!" he said.

6

I Scream for More Clues

The next day Nancy put on a pale purple sweater and her favorite pair of jeans. She put her blue notebook in her back pocket. As she was brushing her reddish blond hair, she gazed into the mirror and said, "Daddy's right. All I have to do is ask. And today that's just what I'll do."

"Nancy," Hannah called from the kitchen. "Come eat these scrambled eggs, or you'll be late for school."

"Coming, Hannah!" Nancy yelled. Then she raced downstairs for breakfast.

Hannah had made such a big breakfast

that Nancy *was* almost late for school. She bounded into her classroom just as the bell rang. She didn't have time to talk to Mrs. Reynolds or Stevie all morning.

At lunchtime Nancy sat with George and Bess. She opened her thermos of vegetable soup and said, "As soon as I get a chance, I'm just going to ask Mrs. Reynolds about Mr. Zuckerman's recipe."

"Well, your chance is walking out the door," George told her. She pointed to the cafeteria entrance. Mrs. Reynolds was leaving, and Stevie Sikes was right behind her.

"Oh, no!" Nancy cried. She jumped up and hurried to the hall monitor. "May I have a pass to Mrs. Reynolds's room, please?" she asked.

When the hall monitor gave her the pass, Nancy raced down the hallway. Then she peeked into her classroom.

Mrs. Reynolds and Stevie were standing over a hot plate. They were both wearing safety goggles. In a beaker, Mrs. Reynolds was heating some of the pink liquid that Stevie had been working on the day before. Nancy could see that crystals had formed in it.

Nancy was just opening her mouth to ask Mrs. Reynolds what they were doing when her teacher spoke. "Great job, Stevie," she said. "This sugary insect food is sure to lure those beetles away from your mother's rose garden. And then you can tell all your classmates what you've been working on."

Nancy's mouth clamped shut. She quietly shut the classroom door.

Stevie and Mrs. Reynolds really *were* working on a science project, she said to herself. I just *knew* my teacher wouldn't ever do anything wrong.

Nancy began to skip back down the hallway to the cafeteria. I can't wait to tell Bess and George, she thought. Then she skidded to a halt.

"Wait a minute," Nancy whispered to herself. "If Stevie and Mrs. Reynolds don't have Mr. Zuckerman's recipe, that must mean that Andrew and Cathy Perez do."

Nancy's happiness drained away. But

then she remembered what her father had said at dinner the night before: "Maybe *nobody* has it."

Daddy's right, Nancy thought. If I'm going to find out what Andrew and Cathy are up to, I'll have to ask them, too. I'll start with Cathy at the Double Dip this afternoon.

Instead of heading back to the cafeteria, Nancy hurried to the school entryway. She dug some coins out of her jeans pocket and called Hannah on the school pay phone.

"Hi, Hannah," she said. "Can I please go back to the Double Dip after school? It's really important."

"You're right," Hannah said, chuckling. "Ice-cream cones *are* important! Don't eat too much and spoil your appetite, though. Mrs. Marvin has invited you and George over for dinner."

"Perfect!" Nancy said. "We'll go home with Bess after the Double Dip. Thanks, Hannah."

Nancy ran back to the cafeteria and sat down with Bess and George.

"Your soup's cold," Bess announced.

"That doesn't matter," Nancy said excitedly. "What does matter is that Mrs. Reynolds and Stevie don't have Mr. Zuckerman's recipe."

She explained to her friends what she'd seen in their classroom's science station.

"Bug food for his mother's rose garden!" George gasped. "Boy, were we wrong."

"Shhh," Nancy said. "We don't want David Berger and those other boys to hear what Stevie's science project is. We should protect his secret."

"Especially since Stevie didn't do anything bad," Bess agreed.

Nancy took her blue notebook out of her pocket and crossed out Mrs. Reynolds's and Stevie's names.

"I just knew Mrs. Reynolds wouldn't do anything mean to Mr. Zuckerman," George said happily.

"But this means we have to go back to the Double Dip after school today and ask Cathy Perez about her new candy," Nancy said.

"Good," Bess said. She looked at Nancy and added, "Then I'll finally get my ice-cream cone!"

After school the girls returned to the Double Dip. When they walked into the store, they were surprised to see Andrew Leoni at the counter again. This time he was buying a bag of chocolate-covered jelly bears.

Nancy, George, and Bess fell into line behind Andrew.

"Yum! Thanks, Cathy," Andrew said. He popped one of the chewy candies into his mouth.

"You're welcome," Cathy said. She hit some keys on the store computer. "Okay, Andrew, after yesterday's triple dip and today's jelly bears, you have five dollars left on your gift certificate. That amounts to several more treats. That was a nice birthday gift your uncle gave you."

Nancy couldn't believe her ears. "Gift certificate!" she cried.

"So, you had nothing to do with the

new candy, Andrew?" Bess blurted, pointing at the glass case of sweets.

"What do you mean?" Andrew asked. His mouth was full of chocolatey jelly candy.

"Yes, how could Andrew have anything to do with our new candy?" Cathy said. "After all, he doesn't work at the dairy."

Nancy stepped up to the counter. "This candy came from the dairy?" she asked Cathy.

"Yes," Cathy said. "You see, the River Heights Dairy usually makes just enough candy to mix into our fun ice-cream flavors."

"Don't I know it," Bess said. She eyed the buckets of ice cream in the freezer case. "I can never decide which flavor is my favorite—Jelly Blast or Chocolate Pretzel Crunch."

"You're right, Bess," Cathy said. "Our candy ice creams are extra popular. So when the dairy told me they'd made too much candy this month, I told them I'd try to sell it here. It's been a big success."

"That's great," Nancy said.

"Yes," Cathy replied happily. "But I don't understand, Nancy. Why did you think Andrew had something to do with the Double Dip's new candy?"

"Well, to tell you the truth," Nancy said, swallowing hard, "you and Andrew were suspects in my latest mystery."

"What!" Andrew and Cathy said together. Andrew stopped chewing on his jelly bears he was so surprised.

"You see, Mr. Zuckerman lost his brand-new secret candy recipe," Nancy began.

"Mr. Zuckerman over at Zuckerman's Zonked?" Cathy asked, looking troubled. "That's too bad. Mr. Zuckerman is a friend of mine."

"I like him, too," Nancy said. "That's why I wanted to find out what happened to the recipe really bad. So when I saw yesterday that you were serving candy, and that you gave Andrew a big ice-cream cone for free . . ."

"You thought I took Mr. Zuckerman's recipe and gave it to Cathy?" Andrew demanded. "I wouldn't do that. Not even for a million scoops of free ice cream!"

"Well, that's what I was coming over here to ask you," Nancy said. "My dad told me the best way to find out the truth is just to ask."

Cathy smiled at the young detective. "You did the right thing, Nancy," she said. "It's always best to ask people directly if they've done something wrong. You were brave to come here today. And I'm happy to say that Andrew and I are innocent."

"I'm happy about that, too," Nancy said, feeling relieved.

"In fact, I think you girls deserve some candy," Cathy added. She opened the glass candy case. "How about it? Would you like some chocolate-covered potato chips? Or some jelly strawberries?"

"No, thank you, Cathy," Nancy said. She walked to the Double Dip's door. "I think we're all candied out."

As soon as the girls had left the ice-cream parlor, George added, "And we're all out of suspects!"

7

A Close Call for Bess

After they left the Double Dip, the girls headed to Bess's house.

"I really hate to disappoint Mr. Zuckerman," Nancy said as they trudged down the sidewalk.

"I know what you mean," Bess agreed. "But I guess your dad's right. Maybe nobody took the secret candy recipe. It's as if it just vanished into thin air."

"Hmm, I don't know," Nancy said. "Things just don't disappear. Especially when you pay close attention to them, the way Mr. Zuckerman did."

"Yeah, remember how he was so careful to put the piece of paper back in his coat pocket?" George said.

"Exactly," Nancy said as the girls turned into Bess's driveway. "It just doesn't add up."

"I guess," Bess said. "But I can't help—Hey, what's that delicious smell?"

Bess opened the front door and bounded into the kitchen with Nancy and George at her heels.

"Hi, Mom," Bess said. "What are you making?"

"Hello, girls!" Mrs. Marvin said. She was just pulling a cookie sheet out of the oven. It was covered with little brown squares. They looked delicious. And they smelled even better.

"I made a surprise for you and your friends, Bess," Mrs. Marvin announced. "Let the candies cool a little bit and then you can try one."

"*More* candy?" Bess shouted. "Yay!"

"Wow, Aunt Anna," George said as she hung her backpack on a kitchen chair. "Those smell great."

"Mm-hmmm," Nancy said. She closed

her eyes and took a deep whiff. "They smell just like . . ."

Suddenly Nancy's blue eyes snapped open. She stared at Bess and said in a trembling voice, "They smell just like maple syrup."

"You're right," George said. She turned to glare at her cousin. "Just like in Mr. Zuckerman's recipe!"

"You don't think *I* took the recipe, do you?" Bess asked. She looked as if she might cry. "I would never steal anything, no matter how scrumptious that recipe sounded."

"Steal something?" Mrs. Marvin said. "Wherever did you get that idea, Nancy? My good friend in Canada just sent me a can of pure maple syrup. So I decided to whip up a new recipe. I'm calling it Chewy Maple Scotcheroos. Here, try one."

"Oh, th-thank you, Mrs. Marvin," Nancy stuttered.

Nancy took a candy from Bess's mother. She nibbled at the sweet, but she was too upset to taste it. She put her candy on the kitchen counter and grabbed Bess's hand.

"I'm sorry Bess," Nancy said. "I know you would never steal something. I just want to help Mr. Zuckerman so badly."

"I understand," Bess said, although she still looked a little hurt. "It's frustrating when a mystery is so tough to solve."

"I'm sorry, too, Bess," George said. She chewed on her Maple Scotcheroo thoughtfully. Then she said, "So what's the *next* step on the candy hunt, Nancy?"

"Well, maybe it's time to face the truth," Nancy said. "Maybe *nobody* has that recipe. Like you said, Bess, it must have just disappeared. And that's what I'll have to tell Mr. Zuckerman—I couldn't solve the mystery."

"Wow," Bess said. "When are you going to tell him, Nancy?"

"I guess I could call him now," Nancy said. She picked up the kitchen phone. Then she hung it up without dialing. She frowned.

"This is hard," Nancy said. "I hate having to tell Mr. Zuckerman that I didn't find his recipe."

"Maybe you'd feel better if you told him in person," George said. "We could go with you to the factory."

"Good idea," Nancy said. She turned to Bess's mother, who was washing the cookie sheet in the sink.

"Mrs. Marvin, could you please drive us to the candy factory?" Nancy asked.

"I think we can do that," Mrs. Marvin said. "We have just enough time before dinner."

On the drive to the factory the girls spoke little. Only Bess said, "I hope Mr. Zuckerman isn't *too* disappointed in us."

In *me,* Nancy thought to herself. I'm the one who was so sure I could solve this mystery.

Mrs. Marvin interrupted her thoughts with an exclamation. "Oh, what a marvelous building, girls!" she said. "It looks just like a stack of—"

"Jelly beans!" George and Bess yelled together.

Nancy couldn't help but giggle at her best friends.

"Glad we could cheer you up a bit," George said with a grin. "Come on, let's go talk to Mr. Zuckerman."

Nancy took a deep breath and walked to the mouth-shaped front door with her friends and Mrs. Marvin.

They went inside and walked to a desk near the door. A secretary was sitting there, typing on a computer.

"May we see Mr. Zuckerman, please?" Nancy asked.

"I'll take you to his office," the secretary said. She led them to a chocolate-colored door. Mr. Zuckerman was writing something at his desk when Nancy stepped into the office. George, Bess, and Mrs. Marvin followed her.

"Ah, it's Nancy Drew, girl detective," Mr. Zuckerman said. He jumped out of his chair and came over to the girls. When he stuck out his arm to shake Mrs. Marvin's hand, Nancy saw a green lollipop dangling from his wrist. Bess saw it, too. She couldn't help plucking it off and chuckling.

"Oh, dear, there's another thing sticking to me!" Mr. Zuckerman exclaimed. "You'll have to forgive me, children. I still haven't rid myself of all that purple goo. Our slogan is 'The Stickiest Goo on Earth!' And *that* has proven to be quite true."

Nancy was gazing at the lollipop in Bess's hand. She frowned in thought. She barely heard Mr. Zuckerman as he went on.

"You know, this whole goo incident has given me an idea," he said. "Tell me what you think, girls—a de-gooer you can eat. I think it could be a big hit with clumsy children and babies."

Suddenly Nancy gasped. Then she said, "I don't mean to interrupt, Mr. Zuckerman, but can you take us to the library?"

8

A Sweet Solution

Mr. Zuckerman looked at Nancy. He semed confused.

"You want to go to the library?" he said. "I don't see why not. You must have some important research to do."

"It *is* important!" Nancy exclaimed. "Let's hurry!"

With Mr. Zuckerman leading the way, the group raced across the factory floor. Then they hurried through the twisty, turny hallway until they came to the library's big, wooden door. Finally they burst into the book-filled room.

Somehow, between the office and the

library, Bess had found a chocolate bar. She was munching it as she said, "What's so important in the library, Nancy?"

Nancy didn't answer. Instead, she stood still for a moment. She gazed at all the bookshelves. Then she bounded over to one of the shelves. She took a familiar-looking recipe book down and examined its front cover. She turned it over and looked at the back cover. Then she flipped through all the pages.

"Hmm," Nancy said. She replaced the book on the shelf. She thought hard and scanned the other bookshelves.

"What is Nancy looking for?" Mr. Zuckerman asked George.

"Search me," George said with a shrug.

Just then Nancy spotted a familiar-looking set of books on a high shelf. They were the chocolate encyclopedias.

"Ah-ha!" she said. She climbed up on a chair and pulled down several of the pretty brown books. Quickly Nancy flipped through the first book. She frowned and moved it aside. Th reached for another volume. She began to turn it over.

"My dear," Mr. Zuckerman offered. "If you want to do some chocolate research, I can help you."

Nancy looked at the back of the book in her hands. Then she grinned.

"No, Mr. Zuckerman," she announced. "You don't need to help me. I just found what I was looking for."

Nancy lifted the last, heavy encyclopedia volume: *Wax Lips–Zoobers*. Then she showed it to the group. They all gasped. Stuck to the back cover of the big book was Mr. Zuckerman's secret candy formula.

"My recipe!" Mr. Zuckerman cried. He dashed over to Nancy and took the book from her. Then he carefully peeled the recipe from the cover.

"Why, it was stuck to the book with a layer of this pesky purple goo!" he exclaimed. "Nancy, I can't thank you enough." Mr. Zuckerman was so happy, he gave the scrap of paper a big, loud kiss.

"That must taste good," Bess said.

"But, Nancy," Mr. Zuckerman said, "how ever did you know where to find my recipe?"

Nancy pointed to Mr. Zuckerman's wrist. "The lollipop that was stuck to your wrist," she said. "I realized if everything was sticking to you, then a piece of paper could stick to you, too."

"True," Mr. Zuckerman said. "But how did the recipe get stuck to the encyclopedia?"

"Remember?" Nancy said. "After you showed us your recipe, you put it back in your coat pocket. Or so you thought. But it must have stuck to your hand. Then, when you put the encyclopedia away, the recipe got stuck to the cover."

"Clever girl," Mr. Zuckerman said. "How can I ever thank you?"

"How about with candy?" Bess piped up.

"Bess!" Mrs. Marvin scolded. "That's not polite."

"Oh, I'm never offended by children who like candy," Mr. Zuckerman said with a smile. "Why don't we take a walk through the factory and pick up some goodies for your ride home."

Then Mr. Zuckerman turned to Nancy. "But a mere goodie bag cannot express my gratitude." Suddenly his face lit up. "I know what I'll do. I'll name my new candy after you! We'll call it Nancy's Mapley Nougat."

"Really? How sweet," Nancy said with a laugh. "Thanks, Mr. Zuckerman."

After Mr. Zuckerman loaded the girls down with Sticky Jelly Bugs, Wacky Fruitz, and Teensy-Tiny Nut 'n' Fluffs, they tumbled into the backseat of Mrs. Marvin's minivan.

Mr. Zuckerman waved goodbye, calling, "I'm going straight to my office to make another copy of this recipe. I won't lose it again. Thank you, Nancy Drew!"

"Wow!" Bess cried, biting into a little marshmallow sandwich. "I knew you could do it, Nancy."

"Yeah," George agreed as she licked a grape-flavored Wacky Fruitz. "That's what I call sweet success."

Nancy pulled out her blue notebook. As

Mrs. Marvin drove, she turned to the missing recipe page. Then she wrote:

I found the missing recipe. But here's the next mystery—what *is* that secret candy that Mr. Zuckerman is working on?

Part of me can't wait to find out. But searching for Mr. Zuckerman's recipe for so long taught me something—good things are worth waiting for. And if I know Zuckerman's Zonked Candy, Nancy's Mapley Nougat is going to be a very good thing, no matter how long I have to wait to taste it!

Case closed.